DESMOND COLE
GHOST PATROL

THE SLEEPWALKING SNOWMAN

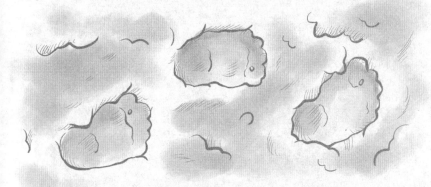

by Andres Miedoso
illustrated by Victor Rivas

LITTLE SIMON

New York   London   Toronto   Sydney   New Delhi

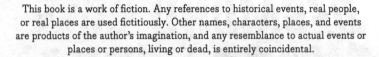

LITTLE SIMON

An imprint of Simon & Schuster Children's Publishing Division
1230 Avenue of the Americas, New York, New York 10020
First Little Simon hardcover edition March 2019
Copyright © 2019 by Simon & Schuster, Inc.
Also available in a Little Simon paperback edition.

For information about special discounts for bulk purchases, please contact
Simon & Schuster Special Sales at 1-866-506-1949 or business@simonandschuster.com.
The Simon & Schuster Speakers Bureau can bring authors to your live event. For more information
or to book an event contact the Simon & Schuster Speakers Bureau at 1-866-248-3049 or
visit our website at www.simonspeakers.com.
Designed by Steve Scott
Manufactured in the United States of America 0219 FFG
2 4 6 8 10 9 7 5 3 1
Library of Congress Cataloging-in-Publication Data
Names: Miedoso, Andres, author. | Rivas, Victor, illustrator.
Title: The sleepwalking snowman / by Andres Miedoso ; illustrated by Victor Rivas.
Description: First Little Simon hardcover edition. | New York : Little Simon, [2019] |
Series: Desmond Cole ghost patrol ; 7 | Summary: Desmond and Andres face a snowman
that was built by a schoolmate but seems to have a mind of its own,
as well as a snowball-throwing bully.
Identifiers: LCCN 2018036952 | ISBN 9781534433472 (paperback) |
ISBN 9781534433489 (hc) | ISBN 9781534433496 (eBook)
Subjects: | CYAC: Snowmen—Fiction. | Winter—Fiction. | Bullying—Fiction. |
Friendship—Fiction. | African Americans—Fiction. |
Hispanic Americans—Fiction. | BISAC: JUVENILE FICTION / Action & Adventure / General. |
JUVENILE FICTION / Readers / Chapter Books.
Classification: LCC PZ7.1.M518 Sle 2019 | DDC [Fic]—dc23
LC record available at https://lccn.loc.gov/2018036952

CONTENTS

CHAPTER ONE

WINTER IS WEIRD

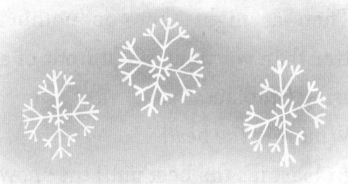

Winter is weird, isn't it?

At first, everything is great! There's a chill in the air. The first snowfall covers the world like a white, fluffy blanket. Even the smell of winter is awesome.

And there are so many things to do:

like snowball fights, skiing, playing hockey, sledding, skating, and even making snowmen.

Then at night there is nothing better than warming up in front of a roaring fireplace.

Winter is *the best*!

At least it's the best until the snow gets all dirty and gross. Then the streets get icy and slippery, and it gets so windy outside, you can't even keep your eyes open.

The days get shorter. It gets dark right after school. And then there's no time for winter fun.

If I thought winter in Kersville was going to be any different, boy, was I wrong.

Big-time!

See, that's me, Andres Miedoso, under all that snow. And that's my best friend, Desmond Cole, with the snowballs.

And that's the sleepwalking snowman. Yeah, you heard me right.

DESMOND COLE

ANDRES MIEDOSO

How did we end up here? Well, like I said, winter is *weird*!

Let me start at the beginning.

OUR SNOWY NIGHTMARE

CHAPTER TWO

A SNOWMAN PROBLEM

It was a perfect winter day. Desmond and I were in his garage, also known as the Ghost Patrol office.

I took a sip of hot chocolate and slurped down one of the warm, melty marshmallows. It tasted ooey-gooey and hot . . . just the way I like it.

"What's that?" I asked, pointing to one of the strange gadgets hanging on his wall.

"It's the Goblin Detector 3000," Desmond said. "But it doesn't work."

My hands started to shake. "G-goblin detector?" I asked.

Desmond smiled. "When I get it to work, we'll be able to find goblins anywhere!"

He was excited about this. Me? I was happy living a goblin-free life!

A knock on the door made me jump.

"Looks like we have a customer!" Desmond said as he opened the door.

A bunch of snow and cold air blew inside. So did a kid, wrapped from head to toe in heavy winter gear.

"Welcome to the Ghost Patrol," Desmond said to the kid.

All we heard was a muffled grunt as the kid unwrapped a super-long scarf.

Underneath the pile of clothes was a boy. I didn't know him, but I had seen him around school.

"My name is Carter James," he said with a scared look in his eyes. "I have a problem."

"Is it a monster problem?" asked Desmond.

Carter shook his head. "No."

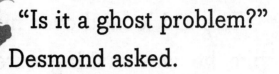

"Is it a ghost problem?" Desmond asked.

"No," Carter said.

I leaned forward and asked, "Is it a *math* problem?"

"No," Carter said.

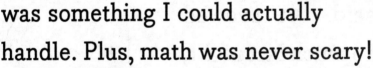

Why can't anyone ever come here with a math problem? I thought. That was something I could actually handle. Plus, math was never scary!

Desmond sat behind his desk. "Tell us what kind of problem you have, Carter."

The kid looked over his shoulder, like he was making sure we were alone. "It's a *snowman* problem," he whispered. "You see, I built a snowman in my yard yesterday. But when I woke up this morning, my snowman was gone."

"That's easy to solve," Desmond said. "It snowed so much last night, your snowman got covered up."

"Nope," Carter said. "That's not what happened."

"Maybe some other kids knocked it down," I guessed.

"Y-you don't understand," Carter said with a shaky voice. "I f-found the snowman."

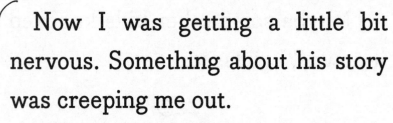

Now I was getting a little bit nervous. Something about his story was creeping me out.

"Well, then, the mystery's solved!" I said. "Sounds like you don't need us."

"I need your help," Carter pleaded.

"My snowman moved to another yard . . . all by itself. Then it vanished. I don't know where it is!"

A walking snowman?

That was all Desmond needed to hear. The Ghost Patrol had a new case!

CHAPTER THREE

TOASTY TOES

Back at my house, I prepared for the snowman mystery.

The secret to battling the freezing cold is wearing layers of clothes. I put on my favorite red sweater, then my red vest, then the blue scarf and hat my mom knitted for me.

Last, but not least, I put on my winter boots. I loved them! They were the thickest, furriest, warmest boots I had ever worn. No matter how slushy and cold it was outside, my toes were always dry and toasty!

The doorbell rang. Of course it was Desmond. He was wearing his Ghost Patrol backpack. That meant he was on the case.

When Desmond stepped inside, he stopped in his tracks and stared at me.

"What?" I asked him. What could take away Desmond's power of speech? It had to be something *big*!

"What's wrong?" I asked again. "Come on, Desmond. Talk to me, man. This isn't funny."

I started to tremble. Was there something behind me? A monster? A mummy? *A goblin?*

I swallowed hard and waited for Desmond's answer, but he just kept staring.

Just then Zax floated into the room through the wall. "Hey, guys," he said. But then he stopped talking and stared at me too. His ghost mouth dropped all the way to the ground!

"Not you, too, Zax!" I screamed. My heart was thumping. "What is everybody staring at?"

Finally, Desmond and Zax looked at each other and burst out laughing.

Zax said, "It's your boots, Andres!"

"Yeah," Desmond said. "They're so . . . furry. Did you steal them from Bigfoot? Or wrestle them away from a bear?"

Zax nodded as he giggled. "Are they still alive?"

"You guys are *the worst!*" I said as my heart slowed to its normal speed. "We'll see who's laughing when my feet are warm and your feet are freezing!"

Zax cackled again. "Dude, I don't even have any feet!"

Okay, that made me laugh too. A lot. Maybe too much.

Desmond cleared his throat. "Are you ready?"

I nodded. It was time to find the missing snowman.

CHAPTER FOUR

SNOWBALL BULLY

Since Zax couldn't stop giggling every time he looked at my boots, Desmond and I decided to leave him at home. After all, we were on a serious mission. No giggling allowed!

Soon we were at Carter's house across from Kersville Park.

Carter yawned big and loud. "Sorry. I couldn't sleep last night." He walked across the yard and stopped near a tree. Desmond and I followed him. The spot was completely empty. "This is where I built the snowman."

Right away, Desmond opened his backpack and got to work. A few minutes later, he had set up some flags and tied yellow tape around that part of the yard. Desmond called it "the Ghost Patrol scene." He really took his job seriously.

Finally, Desmond said, "Carter, tell me about your snowman."

Carter pulled a slip of paper out of his pocket. "Here—I wrote down all the details."

Desmond nodded. I could tell he liked this Carter kid.

After reading the notes, Desmond searched the Ghost Patrol scene, looking for clues. Then he dropped to his knees and pulled out a . . . *ruler*? Desmond Cole had a ton of gadgets in his backpack. Why would he need a ruler of all things?

"Do you see what I see?" Desmond asked, measuring the snow. "Look at these!"

I bent down. When I looked closely, I could see there were foot-prints. They were plain with no boot treads or anything. They looked kind of fluffy, too.

Whoever moved the snowman
must have been lighter than air!

Suddenly something freezing cold hit my head. "Aargh!" I screamed. "What was that?"

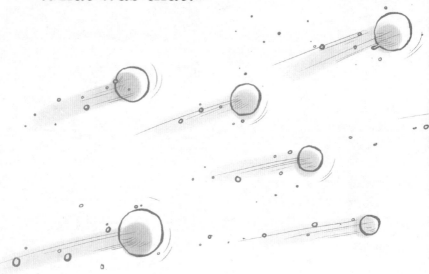

THUD! It hit me again, but this time I knew what it was: *a snowball.*

"Hey!" I yelled, looking around. "That's not cool."

Another snowball hit me on the arm. I ducked down.

"Oh no!" Desmond hollered. "It's Cindy Lee! Run for it!"

Across the street, I saw a little girl with an armful of snowballs pop out from behind a tree. And just like

an automatic pitching machine, she threw those snowballs at us fast and *hard*!

No one had to tell me twice. I ran away. "Who is Cindy Lee?"

"She's the neighborhood snowball bully," said Desmond. "Nobody can win a snowball fight against her. She never misses, and you never see her coming."

We reached the back of Carter's house and everyone stopped to catch their breath.

"Just once," Carter huffed, "I'd love to win a snowball fight against Cindy Lee."

That wouldn't be easy. She hit me with so many snowballs that I looked like a snowman. But thanks to my boots, my toes were still super toasty!

CHAPTER FIVE

THE SNOWDRIFT

We waited, silent and still, listening for signs of the snowball bully. But all we heard was nothing. It was a perfectly quiet winter day.

We peeked our heads out and stared at the park across the street. Cindy Lee was gone.

Desmond waved a plan to us with his hands: He wanted us to split up and check behind all the trees in the park for the missing snowman.

I had a hand signal of my own. It meant *Let's go home and have a cup of hot chocolate!* Unfortunately, nobody understood my signal.

So, we split up and searched the park. Desmond went one way, and Carter went the other. Before I knew it, I was all by myself.

Warm feet or not, I didn't like being alone. Especially when I was looking for someone I didn't really want to find.

Sure, there were other kids and parents in the park, but none of them knew that a snowball bully was on the loose.

I ducked from one tree to the other, expecting Cindy Lee to jump out any second. But I didn't find her anywhere. I started to relax.

That was when a kid on a sled flew by me at top speed. He was moving so fast that I had to jump out of his way. I landed in a huge snowdrift.

"Ow," I moaned, lying there. "That hurt."

Leaning against the snowdrift, I had an idea. I could use this as a fort in case Cindy Lee came back!

I started making snowballs and putting them in a pile. Then I noticed something very weird about my winter fort. It had two huge, snowy feet. Looking up, I saw buttons, a long red scarf, and a black hat.

I stood up, forgetting all about Cindy Lee, and stared at my fort. It had a face . . . with a carrot nose and scary teeth!

I almost screamed. This wasn't a snowdrift. This was the biggest snowman I had ever seen!

It looked so creepy that I waved my arms in front of it to make sure it wasn't alive. The snowman didn't move, but this was Kersville. Almost everything here was haunted. So I did the most logical thing I could think of: I climbed onto the snowman and tried to pull off its carrot nose. I tugged and tugged, but it was frozen in tight.

"Hey, Desmond and Carter!" I yelled. "Come here!"

A few seconds later, Desmond came over alone. "It's just me.

Carter was tired so he went home to get some sleep—Whoa! That's a big snowman. Are you trying to climb to the top?"

"No," I grunted as I planted my feet on the snowman's chest to pull harder. "I'm trying to get this carrot."

Desmond stared at me in awe. "You're weird, Andres. Just let it go. This snowman isn't going anywhere."

CHAPTER SIX

FRIGHTFUL WEATHER

"Do you think this is Carter's missing snowman?" I asked after I climbed down.

Desmond walked around and pulled out the paper that Carter had given him. "There's only one way to find out. We will follow this list."

That made sense to me.

"Are there three buttons?" asked Desmond.

"Check," I said. This snowman had three buttons.

"And a red scarf?"

"Check."

"And a black—"

But before Desmond could finish talking, we heard a strange noise. It sounded like a low groan.

"What was that?" I asked.

Desmond shrugged. "Dunno."

Then we heard it again. But it wasn't a groan. It was a . . . *yawn?*

And it came from the snowman.

The creature lifted its arms high into the air and yawned again.

"The snowman is waking up!" Desmond screamed. "Come on!"

Desmond ran, but I was too scared to move. I was frozen. Well, everything except my toasty toes, but you already knew that.

"Andres," Desmond yelled. "Move!"

The snowman looked down at me and smiled with its scary, jagged teeth. Then it leaned over and let out a sound that came from deep inside all that snow.

It was a *growl*!

I could definitely run then!

The snowman stumbled after us with its arms outstretched. It was trying to snatch us!

Or was it trying to eat us?

Either way, I didn't want to find out.

Desmond and I ran across the park. We jumped over kids on sleds.

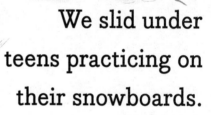

We slid under teens practicing on their snowboards.

We swooped along the cross-country trails, weaving in between skiers.

Nothing was going to stop us!

Nothing . . . until *whack*!

A snowball hit the side of my face.
Cindy Lee was back!

Whack! Whack!

"Ow!" Desmond and I screamed
as snowballs crashed all around us.

Cindy Lee was hiding behind a tree, and she had a pile of snowballs beside her! We were trapped! If we ran one way, we'd be attacked by a snowball bully. But if we ran the other way, we'd be eaten by a snowman monster.

Desmond and I nodded at each other. There was only one thing to do. We ran toward Cindy Lee!

And nobody could have been more surprised than Cindy Lee herself. She pelted us with snowballs until she saw the overgrown snowman chasing us. Her eyes widened bigger than big, and before we knew it, all three of us were running from the snowman *together*.

Actually, Cindy Lee was way faster than we were. She was gone in a flash.

Me on the other hand? I slipped and tumbled into the snow. Hard.

Luckily, we were at the top of an icy hill, and I slid down it on my back.

"Great idea!" Desmond called as he leaped into the air headfirst. He slid down the hill on his belly and caught up to me.

Then we glided onto the crowded ice rink at the bottom of the hill. We kept sliding until we crashed right into a heating lamp.

I closed my eyes, waiting to be grabbed by that snowman. But nothing happened.

So I opened my eyes just in time to see the snowman. It was still at the top of the hill, looking down at us. Its stare sent shivers through my body.

But it didn't come after us anymore. Instead, it turned around and walked back into the woods.

CHAPTER SEVEN

WAKE UP

For the first time ever, Desmond Cole didn't chase after a creepy monster. "Let's go back to Carter's house to check out the Ghost Patrol scene," was all he said.

On the way there, I kept checking for that snowman.

I was still in shock. *Did a snow-man just come to life and chase us?* It was too crazy to be real.

The good thing was that the snow-man wasn't following us anymore. Plus, Cindy Lee was scared away. We were safe . . . for now.

Back at the Ghost Patrol scene, Desmond studied the area inside the yellow tape even more carefully now. "I must have missed something," he told me.

I sniffled. Being pelted with snow-balls and chased in the cold air had given me a runny nose. I needed a tissue. *Fast!*

"I'll be right back," I said as I ran to Carter's front door.

After a few knocks, Carter answered, still looking super sleepy. I must have woken him.

"Did you solve the case yet?" he asked.

"No, not yet, but we found your snowman," I said.

I could feel my snot turning into an icicle. "Do you have a tissue?"

"Sure. Yeah. Come in," Carter said. "There are tissues in the kitchen."

He went to get them, and while he was gone, I looked outside the window. Desmond was walking around with a flashlight strapped to his head.

He was carrying a new gadget, something I had never seen before. This was a strange one. It was a box that glowed, and it had a bunch of antennas pointing in different directions. Every few seconds, it changed color.

Now what was that?

Then something else caught my eye. The branches in the trees next to Carter's house were shaking, and a bunch of squirrels darted into the yard. As the furry critters passed Desmond, a white blob slipped out into the light.

It was the snowman!

Desmond was so focused on that glowing gadget that he didn't even know the snowman was there.

"Look out!" I yelled. But there was no way he could hear me from inside the house. I had to think fast!

That was when I got an idea. If I splashed that snowman with hot water, it would be melt-ville for that giant snowball for sure.

"Carter!" I yelled as I raced down the hall. "I need a thermos!"

In the kitchen, I found Carter completely asleep at the table. "Wake up," I said, shaking him. "I need a thermos. I have to melt your snowman. Fast!"

But I couldn't wait for Carter to wake up. I looked around the kitchen, found a few on my own, and filled them with hot water.

As I ran back outside, I could hear Carter waking up. "What's going on?" he muttered. "Andres, wait!"

But I wasn't going to wait. I had to save Desmond!

Except when I opened the front door and ran into the yard, the snow-man was gone.

Desmond looked up from his weird device, which was glowing orange. He pointed to the thermoses. "Did you make me some tea?"

"Huh?" I asked. I was too busy searching the yard. "The snowman was here just a minute ago."

Desmond said, "I didn't see any-thing."

I wondered if it could have been all in my imagination, but the evidence was right there: giant footprints in the snow.

"Desmond, look!" I said, pointing. "See! The snowman *was* here!"

That was when Carter came outside and walked sleepily across the snow.

"Guys," he said, rubbing his eyes. "I just had the *weirdest* dream."

CHAPTER EIGHT

THUMPETY-THUMP-THUMP

Carter made us come back inside on account of he wasn't wearing his shoes. We went to his room. It was covered in posters of snowboarders and skiers and speed skaters. He even had a sled on the wall next to posters of igloos and . . . snowmen!

"Wow," I said. "You really love winter, don't you?"

"Oh yeah," Carter said, smiling. "It's my favorite season."

"Never mind that," Desmond said impatiently. "Put on your shoes and tell us about your dream so we can go find that snowman."

"You were in it, Desmond," Carter said. "And so were you, Andres. It was so strange. In the dream, I was chas-ing both of you

when all of a sudden, we were all snowball-attacked by Cindy Lee. But for some reason, I didn't run away from her. I stood up to her. And *she* ran away from *me*! Weird, right?"

"Wait," I said. "That happened in real life. Only you weren't the one chasing us. The snowman was! You were dreaming something that really happened."

"That's impossible," Desmond said.

"As impossible as ghosts, monsters, and zombies?" I asked, because I had seen it all in Kersville! "I might know what's going on here," I said. "Have you ever heard of a golem?"

Both Desmond and Carter shook their heads.

"There is a golem in one of my video games," I told them. "You see, golems are these creatures that are made out of, like, mud or clay. But then they come to life and have to do whatever the person who made them wants them to do."

"I don't get it," Desmond said. "The snowman is made of snow, not mud or clay."

"Maybe snow works the same way," I suggested.

Carter yawned. "Do you think I'm controlling the snowman?"

I shrugged. "Maybe? I don't know how it all works. This is just a guess."

Desmond still looked confused. "Why would Carter make the snowman chase after us?"

This was the first time I knew something Desmond didn't. "Golems aren't all that smart," I explained.

"They do what you want, but they
like to do things their own way."

Desmond and Carter still looked
like they didn't understand.

So I continued talking. "Carter needed us to help him with his problem," I said. "Maybe the snowman thought it needed to *catch* us!"

Carter shook his head and yawned again. "But I didn't tell the snowman to do anything! I promise. You've been with me this whole time. And I wasn't even around to see the snowman."

That got me thinking. Every time we saw the snowman come to life, Carter was home . . . asleep.

"That's it!" I said, clapping my hands. "The snowman is sleepwalking! And, Carter, you're controlling it when you sleep. That's why you've been having such weird dreams."

Finally, Desmond nodded and turned to Carter. "Yes! Andres is right. Let's see what happens if you take a nap for a little while."

"I *am* pretty sleepy," Carter said. "I'll just lie down for a few minutes."

He climbed into his bed, and he was fast asleep in no time.

Desmond and I stood there, not sure what to expect. A few seconds later, we heard something from downstairs.

THUMPETY-THUMP-THUMP!

The sound was getting closer.

And closer.

THUMPETY-THUMP-THUMP!

Suddenly, Carter's bedroom door swung open.

The sleepwalking snowman had found us!

CHAPTER NINE

CATCH ME IF YOU CAN

I heard a scream. And then another. And then another! But of course, it was only me screaming.

The snowman blocked the whole doorway. It was impossible to escape.

Desmond yelled, "Let's wake up Carter and stop him from dreaming!"

We shook Carter, but it was no use. That kid could sleep!

The snowman entered the room, creeping closer and closer.

I swallowed hard. "Remember, Carter doesn't want to hurt us, so the snowman won't hurt us."

Then the snowman launched a snowball that hit me square in the face.

Splat!

Desmond cleared his throat. "I thought it didn't want to hurt us."

"Maybe I was wrong," I said as the snowman loomed over us with its arms outstretched. "Haven't you ever been wrong before?"

I screamed again and waited for the snowman to grab us.

But before that could happen, Desmond grabbed the sled from Carter's wall.

"Get behind me," Desmond said, holding the sled in front of us like a shield.

The snowman pelted the sled with snowballs.

"Let's get out of here!" Desmond cried.

We moved around the snowman, then bolted out of the room, down the stairs, and through the front door at top speed. As soon as we hit the yard, we both hopped onto the sled. We had to get away from there!

Only we didn't get far.

In a flash, the snowman jumped out of Carter's bedroom window and landed right in front of us. It was quick for a pile of snow!

"Hold on tight," Desmond said, swerving around the frozen beast.

The sled was fast, but the snow-man was faster. *Much* faster! He was so fast that it seemed to be skating on the snow!

The snowman reached out to grab me, but it ended up with just a piece of my scarf. "Let go!" I screamed. No way was I going to give up the scarf my mom made for me!

So I tugged it back and almost fell off the sled. Desmond held me as we picked up speed.

"Where are we going?" I asked Desmond, wiping the snow from my eyes.

"We need to find Cindy Lee," he said. "I have a plan."

Desmond Cole *always* had a plan!

We flew into the park, weaving in and out of the trees. Desmond and I looked back and saw that the snow-man was still chasing us.

"What's the plan?" I asked as we hit a hill and slid down it.

"Remember when Carter said he always wanted to win a snowball fight against Cindy Lee?" Desmond asked. "Well, I bet if the snowman sees Cindy Lee, it will stop chasing us and fight with her!"

That was a great idea . . . with only one problem. *We* didn't find Cindy Lee. Cindy Lee found *us*! Which meant we were stuck between a snowball bully and a sleepwalking snowman again!

Thwack!

"Owww!" I screamed as Cindy Lee bombarded us with snowballs. That girl had some kind of aim.

Luckily, Desmond's plan worked.

When the sleepwalking snowman saw Cindy Lee, it froze. What came next was the most epic snowball fight in history.

It was so awesome that Desmond and I stopped sledding so we could watch.

At first, the snowman had the upper hand, but then Cindy Lee came roaring back. As the snowballs hurled across the park, Desmond whispered to me, "Andres, give me your boots."

"Are you really going to make fun of my boots at a time like this?" I snapped.

"No way," Desmond said. "We need your boots now more than ever. Please?"

I sighed, then I took off my boots and handed them over to him. My dry, warm toes were now super cold and wet. This new idea had better be a good one.

Desmond snuck over behind the snowman. There was no way the creature was going to notice him. It was too busy flinging snowballs at Cindy Lee.

Then Desmond set my boots on the ground.

As the snowman dodged the snow-balls, it stepped into my boots, and it must have been like stepping into the sun.

That snowman started to sweat like crazy. Then I realized that it wasn't sweating.

It was *melting*!

It didn't take long before the snow-man was nothing more than a large puddle.

Cindy Lee stopped throwing snow-balls as I ran over to get my boots. *Oof! Gross!* They smelled like wet dog.

My poor, toasty boots were ruined, but the sleepwalking snowman case was solved!

CHAPTER TEN

MELT AWAY

It turns out that all Carter needed was a good night's sleep. His tired grumpiness had turned the snowman into a grumpy golem. But after some rest, Carter was able to build a new, nicer snowman. I know, it sounds crazy. Why build *another* snowman?

Well, because golems can be useful. While the whole town was asleep, Carter had his snowman build a perfect winter park for everyone to enjoy.

We called it the Kersville Winter Wonderland, and it had everything: an ice castle with ice slides, a hot chocolate fountain, an igloo bouncy house, and an icicle cave. There were even lanes for sledding races around the whole place.

Plus, there were forts that were filled with round, fluffy snowballs for snowball fights. They were perfect for throwing. It almost felt good to get hit with one . . . almost.

It was hard to believe that Carter created all of this in his sleep. Talk about wild dreams!

No one knew where the snow forts came from, but no one cared. Now people come from all over to visit Kersville's famous Winter Wonderland—but they have no idea it's a park that was built by a snowman!

Like I said before, winter is *weird*, but I think that's what makes it *the best*!